Katie's London Christmas

JAMES MAYHEW

ORCHARD

For Ruth, Paul,
Daniel and Jacob
DeNaeyer
with love

ORCHARD BOOKS
338 Euston Road, London NW1 3BH
Orchard Books Australia
Level 17/207 Kent Street, Sydney, NSW 2000
First published in 2014 by Orchard Books
ISBN 978 1 40832 641 1
Text and illustrations © James Mayhew 2014
The right of James Mayhew to be identified as the author and illustrator of this book has
been asserted by him in accordance with the Copyrights, Designs and Patents Act, 1988.
A CIP catalogue record for this book is available from the British Library.
1 3 5 7 9 10 8 6 4 2
Printed in China
Orchard Books is a division of Hachette Children's Books,
an Hachette UK company.
www.hachette.co.uk

I<small>T WAS</small> C<small>HRISTMAS</small> E<small>VE</small>, and Katie and Jack were fast asleep at Grandma's house. Outside the snow fell and all was quiet.

"Atchoo!"

Katie and Jack woke up.
"Who sneezed?" said Jack.
"Not me!" said Katie.

"Atchoo-oo!"

"Perhaps it was Grandma,"
said Jack.
"Let's take a look," said Katie.
And they tiptoed downstairs.

Somebody was putting presents under the
Christmas tree, but it wasn't Grandma . . .

"Atchoo-ooo-ooo!"

"It's Father Christmas!" whispered Katie. "I think he has a cold."

Father Christmas blew his nose. "I still have so much to do . . . " he sighed.

"We'll help!" said Katie and Jack.
"You two should be asleep,"
smiled Father Christmas.
"But it would be lovely
to have some helpers . . . "

So Katie and Jack put on their
coats and boots, and followed
Father Christmas outside.

The snow crunched under their feet as Father Christmas led them to his sleigh. Katie and Jack were very excited to meet his reindeer.

When everyone was ready, Father Christmas
gathered the reins and . . . WHOOSH!
Up, up they flew, through the swirling snowflakes.

"Let's take a look at London in the snow,"
said Father Christmas. "Hold on tight!"

They flew over Regent Street, in and out of strings
of Christmas lights that sparkled like colourful stars.

In Covent Garden, the last few people were hurrying home
for Christmas after an evening at the ballet.
Katie and Jack waved to some carol singers trying to keep
warm, and ballerinas dancing in the snow.

As they flew over Trafalgar Square, Katie and Jack saw a dazzling Christmas tree. They waved to the big bronze lions . . . and they were sure one of them waved back!

Then they swooped over the Houses of Parliament
and flew twice around Big Ben, just for fun!
"This is fantastic!" shouted Katie.
"More! More!" laughed Jack.

"Atchoo-oo!"

sneezed Father Christmas.

Then, Father Christmas steered the sleigh to some distant rooftops.

"Time to deliver some presents," he said, blowing his nose.

"How will we get down the chimneys?" asked Katie.

"A little bit of Christmas magic," chuckled Father Christmas.

When they landed, Father Christmas clapped his hands.
The air around them sparkled, and Katie and Jack found
themselves floating down the chimney.

Father Christmas showed them how to leave
presents without waking anyone up . . .

And then they dashed from street to street, and roof to roof,
whizzing up and down chimneys big and small,
delivering presents to all kinds of houses . . .

"And now the very last house on my list . . . "
said Father Christmas, with a twinkle in his eye.
"Can you guess where?"
"Oh, please tell us!" said Katie and Jack.

They swept over St James's Park, high over
Horse Guards Parade and down The Mall.
"There it is," chuckled Father Christmas.
Katie and Jack gasped, "Buckingham Palace!"

Father Christmas sorted out the presents and then
chose one of his favourite palace chimneys.
"Are you ready?" he asked.
"Oh, yes!" said Katie and Jack.

They whizzed down the royal chimney and, when Katie opened her eyes, they were by a grand fireplace. There were no stockings, so they looked for a Christmas tree.

There before them stood a huge Christmas tree, and
underneath were lots of royal dogs, sleeping peacefully.
"Shhh," whispered Father Christmas.
"We don't want to wake the corgis."

But then his nose began to twitch.

"Oh, no . . . I think I'm going to . . .

Atchoo-oo!"

At once, all the dogs woke up.

They began to sniff the royal presents.

"Look! Some are shaped like bones!" giggled Katie.

"They must be presents for the dogs," laughed Jack.

Woof!

Woof!

Woof!

Woof!

"Is anyone there?" called a regal-sounding voice.

A door began to open . . .

"Oh, no!" said Father Christmas. "We mustn't be seen. Quick!"

They left all the presents by the tree and ran to the fireplace.

"Here goes," said Father Christmas.

The air sparkled and – just in time – up, up, up they flew.

It had stopped snowing, and the sky was full of stars
as they galloped up into the air, homeward bound.
"All done for another year," yawned Father Christmas.
"Time for a rest."

Soon, they were safely back at Grandma's house.
"Farewell, my friends, and thank you," said Father Christmas
as he flew away into the starlit sky.
"Get well soon!" called Katie and Jack. And, as they
waved goodbye, they heard one last faraway

"Atchoo-oo-ooo!"

Katie and Jack took off their snowy coats and tiptoed upstairs. They were so tired they were soon fast asleep.

When Christmas morning dawned, Grandma had to wake them up. "Come on, you two," she said. "It's Christmas Day! There are presents waiting to be opened!"

Katie and Jack had lots of lovely gifts.

But the very last one left under the Christmas tree
was their favourite.

It was a beautiful London snow globe.

The little note attached read:

"For my wonderful helpers. Merry Christmas, from F. C."

the end